SEVENFOLD

ILYAN KEI LAVANWAY

Cocoa, Florida
USA

ISBN-10: 0615904580
ISBN-13: 978-0615904580

Published by Ilyan Kei Lavanway
Cocoa, Florida, USA

Sevenfold

Dedicated to my mother, who introduced me to the books
that inspired this short story.

CONTENTS

PREFACE

Parts of this short story were inspired by the John M. Pontius book, Visions of Glory, and the W. Cleon Skousen book, The Cleansing of America. Both of the above mentioned books are highly recommended and relevant.

In the near future, the United Nations have become the enforcement arm of the New World Order. What was once the United States of America has been absorbed into the North American Superstate that includes Canada and Central America. Against unspeakable odds, freedom loving people have gathered and built up Zion Cities.

Dozens of Zion Cities located strategically throughout the Western Hemisphere have taken decades to erect. Most are still under construction, facing continual opposition from external forces. Small, self governing bands of Christians have migrated, mostly on foot, seeking refuge in these cities.

CHAPTER ONE

G racie smiled. Her amber eyes sparkled in the sunlight streaming through the kitchen window. A hint of lemon fragrance tickled her nose as she squeezed dish soap onto the sponge. She sang to herself, her voice a whisper. A tattered backpack, a heavily scuffed, fully automatic AR-15 assault rifle with broken bayonet still affixed, and a pair of severely nicked kukri swords, their leather sheaths cracked and torn, leaned against the cabinet doors near the refrigerator.

The life-size display on the refrigerator immersed Gracie in time one year ago to the day. A solitary temple spire glistened in morning rays. Her white wedding dress seemed almost too bright to behold against lush Saint Augustine grass. Hope rekindled. Gracie yearned for a return to newlywed innocence.

We've traveled so far, endured so, so much. Cherish this.

Her mouth watered at the sweet tartness of strawberry cheesecake. The firm warmth of Abiathar's hand engulfed her hand. Her heart leapt as he smiled at her.

Eternity. Will it be long enough for him to enjoy me, and me him? Long enough for us to discover each other? Long enough to enjoy posterity?

Beads of sweat ran down her brow and mixed with tears welling up in her eyes. The thermometer near the kitchen window indicated an outdoor temperature of 105 degrees Fahrenheit, unusually hot for early April in what was once Independence, Missouri. Stranger still was the silence outside. No birds chirping. No dogs barking.

Gracie finished the dishes and dried her hands, wiped her brow and rubbed away her tears. She turned and bent down. From the dusty backpack, she took a few dented cans of what was left of their food storage and set them on the counter near the stove. The labels had long since disintegrated.

Wisdom in small and simple things.

She had heeded her late mother's voice of experience. Having scratched the name of the contents of each can into the lids with the tip of a knife on the date of acquisition, she chose dinner.

As she walked out of the kitchen and into the living room, the display on the refrigerator faded to its normal satin finish. A sigh escaped her throat as she sat down on the sofa and leaned back to relax.

Finally, we're here. Heal, renew, and replenish.

The Urim wall in the living room opened a panoramic view, as if it were a portal into the recently completed conference center. The conference center in New Jerusalem, Jackson County, Missouri, was several times larger than the one in Salt Lake City, Utah. This was the first year Gracie and Abiathar had seen it. Their arduous southward trek had occupied their entire first year of marriage. Surviving like pioneers of old made for an adventurous honeymoon. Blisters on their feet were still healing, as were profound wounds of the soul.

CHAPTER TWO

Atop the Tricentennial Standard-of-Liberty Memorial near city center, a gargantuan American flag rippled in long, flowing surges, like a massive sail on a great ship propelled by strong yet gentle gusts. Few dared fly the Stars and Stripes these days. New Jerusalem was one of the rare places left on the continent where freedom loving people could gather and live the principles of the Constitution independently from the federal socialist government that had taken root almost immediately after November, 2008.

Gracie sat up and scooted to the edge of the sofa, eyes wide with wonder. The prophet, Kenneth F. Thomas, walked onto the stand inside the new conference center. His kind eyes twinkled. The reverent smile gracing his masculine, clean-shaven face hid the weightiness of the responsibilities he bore. Not saying a word, he handed a note to one of the twelve apostles.

After reading the note, the apostle folded it twice and placed it in the inner breast pocket of his suit jacket. He gave a slight nod to the prophet. Those seated in the congregation fidgeted and glanced at each other. Some whispered. Others bowed the head. Still others gazed forward, fixated on the general authorities filing onto the stand. Black suits. White, pressed shirts. Shoes shined to a mirror finish. Close trimmed hair and clean countenances. Firm handshakes. Arms extended in fellowship. Each man sanctified in crucibles of adversity, a stalwart ensign more precious than gold.

Civilization, at long last.

Gracie rubbed her bare feet in the lush carpet of their new home as she listened to the prelude music. Her heart pounded. This would be her first opportunity to experience an entire conference session since she and Abiathar had arrived. They had slept through the morning session. Anticipatory chills coursed down her spine, contrasted by steadfast warmth in her bosom.

Finally, the clock struck two. The Sunday afternoon session of the April, 2077 semiannual General Conference of the Church of Jesus Christ of Latter-day Saints commenced.

CHAPTER THREE

Abiathar listened from the garage. Over black, threadbare tactical pants, a pair of 9mm Glock-17 Gen8 handguns resided, one on each leg. He was awake. They were part of his attire. Acquired habits die hard. He had not been here long enough to shed caution. He had Gracie to protect.

His black outer shirt clung to his back. Wiping his brow, he adjusted the fan mounted on the wall before him.

We needed a reboot. Sure got one. So much work to be done.

Eyes closed, ears open, hands moving with fluid precision, he reassembled his 7.62mm sniper rifle. A thorough manual cleaning was long overdue. He had exhausted his last barrel-mounted, knurled steel vial of nanotech smart cleaner weeks ago.

Task completed, he reattached the frayed shoulder strap to the weapon and hung it over a nail beside his oak workbench. Reaching to his right, he grabbed one of his kukri swords and pulled it from the remnants of its sheath, looked it over, frowned, and shoved it back.

Sharpen you later. Your twin's busted. Saved Gracie, though.

For a brief moment, he choked back great, heaving sobs, thankful Gracie was in the other room. He did not want her to see him like this. Trauma of the past year inundated his soul like a flash flood, now that he had a home and time to process it all.

Above his workbench, a 2045 calendar hung open to the month of August. On it was circled a date, August 30. Across the date was scribbled the faded autograph of Abiathar's grandpa, along with three words that were no longer legible. Abiathar reflected on that memento often. He knew exactly what it meant, but he would not talk about it.

Wish I could've been there with ya, Gramps. What an experience that must've been, meeting all of them and receiving instructions for the days now unfolding.

While listening to General Conference, Abiathar couldn't help but tinker. He took the screws out of the side panel of an iconic monolith, exposing the motherboard. Bouts of sneezing overcame him as dark brown dust floated up from the innards of the Intel Core i29 sixty-four core relic.

And here we have... a collection of parts constituting one of the last silicon-based microprocessor computers.

Modern, quantum processor based devices were not designed for do-it-yourself enthusiasts. In fact, tampering with any consumer device was considered a violation of intellectual property rights. That constituted a felony as far as laws outside New Jerusalem were concerned.

Obscure, second hand parts traders, accessible only by word of mouth and clever bartering through various middle men, afforded Abiathar the needed materials. Memories flooded his mind. Color vacated his expressionless countenance. The trek from Toronto, Ontario, Canada had been riddled with near lethal encounters as he had pursued his obsession along the way.

He glanced at his left hand, at the conspicuous gap between his pinky and his middle finger. He had not bartered them away. They were taken from him. His gold ring, loot. His finger, a morsel for black-toothed outlanders. Only by the grace of God and the power of the priesthood had the gangrene healed. Only by the same had he retained his bride, and her, her virtue.

Frustrated by en route bartering woes and the ever-challenged duty to remain daisy side of dirt, Abiathar chased the dream of assembling a machine capable of crunching archaic data from federally prohibited, encrypted annals of the World Wide Web. Archives were stored in legacy servers outside the jurisdiction of the dozens of Zion Cities that had been constructed over the past few decades.

Urim walls, found exclusively within Zion Cities, could not be used for personal curiosities. Though serious about his fascination with old-school tech and American history, Abiathar made it his personal challenge to do his cyber sleuthing the old fashioned way. Sort of like having access to the latest automotive advancements, but insisting on the nostalgia of American muscle cars.

CHAPTER FOUR

Abiathar plugged the power chord into the wall outlet. *Moment of truth.*

The subtle whir of case fans accompanied by the familiar beep of a power-on-self-test rewarded Abiathar's diligence. The organic LED screen cast its bluish glow. As the boot screen went through its drama, Abiathar reflected on the conditions of his world.

What was it like when you were my age, Gramps? Wish we could have us a good chat. Guess we'll be seein' each other soon enough.

With the exception of Zion Cities, the North American Superstate fell under ruthless international martial law, policed primarily by Chinese, North Korean, Iranian, and Russian soldiers. Outside Zion Cities, law enforcement was funded largely by Saudi Arabia.

Sharia law was ubiquitously enforced. It took root in what was once Oklahoma and spread like cancer over the Western Hemisphere. Public stonings and beheadings were common. Grandpa had witnessed many in person and had nearly lost his life trying to prevent them.

In the outlands, children were trafficked as commodities. Rampant, federally funded abortions drove the trading value of live child slaves skyrocketing. Dead ones were price fixed, as long as they were fresh and intact. A specimen missing appendages and organs mandated deep discounts.

Non-compliant children were tried as adults, especially when their crimes included converting to Christianity. News of social atrocities seldom made it to New Jerusalem.

People in Zion Cities knew the score without being told. Most had spent months or years migrating thousands of miles on foot and had witnessed firsthand what the outside world had become.

Dogs! Impenitent, degenerate outlanders, Gadianton socialists, worshippers of Molech. Your postpartum inventory dwindles, so you turn on our unborn to seal your Luciferian oaths, to indulge your lust for power. I don't know what's worse, you, or those who enabled you to get where you are and do what you do.

Moroni-esque indignation vexed Abiathar's soul frequently. He had observed far too many otherwise upstanding local clergy and community pillars campaign for charismatic and seemingly altruistic despots, deceitful vermin directly responsible for conditions spoken of in prophetic warnings. It was all he could do to school his feelings. He knew in whom he trusted, and he could hardly wait for Him to ass-kick on behalf of the penitent and downtrodden.

Abiathar and Gracie found Conference edifying. Most of what they heard was already familiar to them. Some of it was not. Near the end of the session, Gracie felt her baby kick. She got up to use the toilet.

The apostle conducting the session was last to speak. He stood at the podium, quoted the prophet's note verbatim from memory, and then sat down without further comment. Conference adjourned.

Holding her round belly, Gracie shuffled back to the living room, eyes downcast. Her disappointment over having missed the final remarks and closing hymn and benediction vanished. Something caught her attention.

CHAPTER FIVE

"Abiathar, look!" exclaimed Gracie. Queuing off her piqued emotion, the sound turned up. The scene in which the news commentator stood, though hundreds of miles away, seemed to unfold right outside the house. Gracie felt the hot breeze as if it were blowing through the house unobstructed by the presence of the solid wall.

"Update to breaking news from WNN's New York correspondent, Niles Martin. Niles."

Abiathar hurried in from the garage. He zeroed in on the Urim wall, standing with feet shoulder width apart, fists clenched as he absorbed the commentator's broadcast.

"Dr. Carlson of the World Astronomical Society just announced at a United Nations emergency summit on climate change that solar activity is increasing catastrophically. World leaders and celebrities are rushing to underground shelters. At this point, there seems to be no regard for the panic this news has caused. Dr. Carlson, what kind of solar flare is this? How will it affect us?"

"Niles, this is no flare. We've never seen activity like this. We don't know what to make of it, but it's bad. Solar luminosity is increasing at a linear rate of fifty percent above nominal every twelve hours. Normal variance is plus or minus one tenth of one percent over an eleven year cycle."

"When did this begin, Doctor?"

"Twenty-four hours ago, Niles. Hence, the emergency summit meeting."

"Looks like pandemonium in the streets outside the lobby windows, Doctor."

Superheated glass caught a surge of cold air from the air conditioning system and fractured, emanating thunderous cracking sounds, evoking screams from folks milling around inside the UN building lobby. Shards broke away from upper level windows.

Behind Dr. Carlson, a news camera caught a burst of pink mist. More screams erupted. Outside, a man stopped mid-stride, looking down at what appeared to be his shadow extending ahead of him. The light was in front of him. The hour was not late enough in the day for a man to cast a six-foot shadow. In one hand he carried a hardshell attache case. His hand relinquished its grasp.

The briefcase fell to the ground and bounced forward twice before coming to rest near the man's fallen half. Urine and bile and blood spilled onto the spalling concrete and flashed to vapor, making distinctive sizzling and popping sounds. His upright half, split head to groin, stood stuck to an enormous shard of glass wedged vertically into a crevice in the concrete, displaying internal anatomy as picture perfect as a full color medical textbook.

Onlookers expelled the contents of their stomachs as they looked through the glass and watched the man's beating heart slow to a stop. His eye twitched in its socket and remained wide open. Wet, gurgling noises came from his bisected mouth and nose as his final breath escaped his deflating lung.

"That's an understatement, Niles. The sun's brightness has doubled. By this time tomorrow it'll be triple its normal brightness. Quadruple by the day after tomorrow. People are panicking. The Information Transparency Division has implemented rolling blackouts on all personal communications. This will be followed by an indefinite and total communications shut down as soon as key officials and their significant others are secured."

"Dr. Carlson, what about the rest of us?"

"Frankly, Niles, we've been hung out to dry. Severe drought will grip the world. Lakes will evaporate. Rivers will dry up. Oceans will overheat, killing marine life. If this persists, oceans will vanish and rocks will melt. Earth's crust will eventually become a shell of glass with minimal topography. In short, Niles, we're f..."

Dr. Carlson fell, dead.

Abiathar spoke to Gracie without looking at her. He was still fixated on the newscast. "I know, Hun. I got that relic up and running. Found some stuff you've gotta see. I've been following this on a banned 'conspiracyparanormal' weblog that some old guy with a weird name still operates underground. There's a lot the media refuses to cover. They won't mention any of the Zion Cities as places of refuge. Or the fact that this, this solar anomaly thing that's happening, its effects are worse in areas concentrated right outside every Zion... City..."

As if his thought process dropped into slow motion, the realization dawned on him. Something was going on outside *this* Zion City.

"No, Dear, I mean look, there, the sky!" Gracie gasped.

Only now did Abiathar notice Gracie had not been watching the news but listening to it as she stared out the front door, her back to the Urim wall. She had been trying to tell him.

CHAPTER SIX

A biathar did an about face and rushed to Gracie's side. He stared, speechless.

A dense cumulonimbus cloud billowed out of thin air, pushing upward as if to extend into space. Its protective shadow and cool torrents cast themselves over the entire city of New Jerusalem. Stark delineation concentrated the storm's ferocity. A massive column of rain enshrouded the city, bounded as abruptly as a wall precisely at city limits.

Abiathar took Gracie by the hand and led her outside. Swelling rivulets coursed down the street, soothing their blistered feet. Neighbors joined them. Some laughed. Some cried. Others stood silent, arms outstretched, eyes shut tight, mouths gaping wide to catch marble sized raindrops. The huge, pelting drops hurt.

Smiles and laughter faded. Solemnity filled each soul as everyone began to comprehend the gravity of the broader scene. All eyes gazed down the gentle slope of the street and beheld, just beyond the edge of town, the blinding glint of the scorching day. Like an undulating, incandescent filament between ground and cloud, shimmering mirages laced with faint wisps of ashen gray blurred everything outside the city.

Gracie shivered. Refreshing downdrafts dragged cold air from the stratosphere. Seismic growl of thunder and relentless pounding of precipitation drowned out clamors of panic and howls of death ensuing beyond the perimeter of town. Copious downpour renewed air over the city, sparing the inhabitants of New Jerusalem from the stench of smoldering flesh and burnt hair and clothing.

In the outlands surrounding the city, charred meat fell off bones as sinews snapped and skin flaked away from the naked, writhing doomed. Tongues stripped of utterance seared in skull ovens. Saliva flashed to steam. Brain and spinal cord boiled in their own fluids. Enamel cracked off teeth. Eyeballs bulged and ruptured like ripe zits, hurling vitreous gel from sockets with projectile force.

No manmade scene of carnage could begin to compare with the cauterizing of a wounded world hemorrhaging virtue and liberty. Had God begun to answer the prayer of a mourning earth witnessed by Enoch?

"Abiathar, what did that apostle say at the end of General Conference?" Gracie shouted above the wind and rain.

Abiathar looked at her, a youthful grin plastered across his drenched face. Ever the gallant romantic, he held her close with his right arm around her slight shoulders, shielding her forehead with his right hand. Puppy-dog eyes looked up at him from beneath matted bangs. Her question lingered through parted lips. She took his breath away.

After a long pause, shedding tears of gratitude indistinguishable from rainwater, Abiathar mustered utterance nothing short of an apostolic voice for all to hear: "The apostle quoted Isaiah 30:26, 'Moreover the light of the moon shall be as the light of the sun, and the light of the sun shall be sevenfold, as the light of seven days, in the day that the Lord bindeth up the breach of his people, and healeth the stroke of their wound.' "

###

ABOUT THE AUTHOR

Ilyan Kei Lavanway is a Christian. He has a youthful exuberance about the Creation and Christian eschatology. He is deeply interested in learning to understand and worthily participate in the fulfillment of prophecies and events of the upcoming days preceding and following the Second Coming of Jesus Christ.

Mr. Lavanway served as a full time missionary for two years in the Argentina Buenos Aires North Mission of the Church of Jesus Christ of Latter-day Saints, 1986 to 1988.

Mr. Lavanway is a United States citizen and a patriot. He loves his country and the U.S. Constitution as envisioned by the Founding Fathers. Mr. Lavanway served on active duty in the U.S. Air Force for almost 14 years in various non-flying operational and academic assignments.

While he never flew for the Air Force, he has always harbored a passionate interest in aviation. Since his circumstances over the past two decades have made it impractical for him to fly, Mr. Lavanway has taken up writing and discovered that he loves it almost as much as he loves flying airplanes.

Connect with the author.

Amazon author page:
http://www.amazon.com/author/ilyan

Goodreads author page:
http://www.goodreads.com/ilyan

Smashwords author page:
https://www.smashwords.com/profile/view/ilyan

Facebook:
https://www.facebook.com/ConspiracyParanormal

LinkedIn:
http://www.linkedin.com/in/ilyanlavanway

Twitter:
https://twitter.com/ilyanlavanway

Blogs:
http://ebooksscifi.wordpress.com

http://conspiracyparanormal.blogspot.com

Websites:
http://ilyanlavanway.wix.com/books

http://conspiracyparanormal.com